THE TRAIL TO
NOWHERE

TED SHUTTLESWORTH

The Trail to Nowhere

ISBN 978-1-7336042-9-1

www.tedshuttlesworth.com

Hill Cottage Publications

Printed in the United States of America

CONTENTS

INTRODUCTION

It would seem that the Old West has been woven into the fabric of America. Those who dwelt in the eastern states fed upon the stories captured in dime novels which glamorized the western gunslingers and mountain men, and the stories of the men and women who helped shape the western frontier.

In 1860, Eratus and Irwin Beadle published "Beadle's Dime Novels." It was the first series of this kind and each book cost just a dime. Ned Buntline was the most famous of the dime novelists. He gave an image of a tough breed of men that fought for truth, honor and freedom in the Old West.

Buffalo Bill Cody came to prominence through the dime novel and it brought him fame across the Nation.

He began a traveling Wild West show. There were as many as 1,200 people that worked the show over the years. There were many famous Old West characters that joined the show such as Wild Bill Hickok, Texas Jack, Annie Oakley, and prominent First Nations chiefs Sitting Bull and Geronimo.

An interesting note was the story of Buffalo Bill's niece who was healed at the Chicago World's Fair. John Alexander Dowie had built what was called the "Little Wooden Hut" at the Fairgrounds. There he preached and prayed for the sick. Here is the transcript of Dr. Dowie and Sadie Cody as published in the *LEAVES OF HEALING.*

> I have touched the hem of His garment; and I stand before you free. A year ago last September I was taken sick at the World's Fair. Nine months ago I became perfectly helpless. I was attended by four physicians and my uncle Dr. David (brother to Buffalo Bill), an eminent physician in this city. They decided that nothing could be done except put me in a plaster-of-Paris cast. Five of my vertebrae were worse than useless, and an abscess as large as my fist was at the base of my spine...that same day a copy of *LEAVES OF HEALING* fell upon my bed... I was brought

to Chicago and Dr. Dowie prayed for me…I felt new life in me there was no pain or aching; I had really awoke to health.[1]

There was also a reoccurring theme of redemption that held the hearts and minds of the early westerners. My library contains the autobiographies of those early men and women. *The Life of Buffalo Bill by William Cody, Wyatt Earp: Frontier Marshal by Stuart N Lake, and Davy Crockett's Own Story as written by Himself*, to name but a few.

Wyatt Earp died in 1927, and my grandmother read about it in her newspaper in northern Maine. She was about seventeen years old. John Wayne was an extra on the movie sets where Earp came to watch the productions. John Wayne said that Wyatt Earp taught him how to walk and wear a gun and filled his heart with stories of the Old West.

These stories spilled over into America's art, literature, and films. My childhood was filled with books about Daniel Boone and Kit Carson. Television was filled with a steady diet of cowboys, good guys, and bad guys, and an unseen code of right and wrong was

---

1. Lindsay, Gordon; *The Life of John Alexander Dowie*, The Voice of Healing Publishing Company, 1951 pp 137-140

instilled into my generation.

My favorites were *Maverick* with the great James Garner, *Cheyenne* with Clint Walker, *Hopalong Cassidy* starring William Boyd, Roy Rogers and Dale, *Have Gun Will Travel* with Richard Boone and anything with John Wayne in it. There were Saturday mornings with *The Lone Ranger and Tonto*. When I was young I read Zane Grey novels and Louis L'Amour books. These were my boyhood memories.

I have written this novel to blend the code of the West with the power of righteous living which built the timbre of the American people. The story of "Manifest Destiny" has been rewritten by modern historians to mean white supremacy at the cost of all other peoples. This is not so.

The thought of "Manifest Destiny" was actually an agrarian move to populate the uninhabited regions of America to feed and provide for all. There were cowboys who were black who gained fame such as Bill Pickett and Nat Love. The Spanish vaqueros worked the West as early as 1519 and married among the First Nations such as the Apache. Chinese workers helped to build railroads and establish trade on the West coast. The First Nation people were part of the strength of this Nation and played a great role in working with the land. The melting pot of America has always had conflicts and racial tension. The ultimate dream is to live together with love and respect for each other.

The Trail to Nowhere, is my desire to write as accurately as possible the American western story in fictional form but with the ultimate goal to remind us where we came from and help us to cross life's final river with victory!

Ted Shuttlesworth Sr.
Hill Cottage, West Virginia
November, 2023

Chapter One

THE LAST WALK

The cold night wrapped its fingers around the old man with a tight grip. He shuffled through the snow-covered street looking for an inviting light. He felt frostbite stinging his face and warmth quickly draining from his body. He had made it to town. The map of the gold mine, which was tucked in his pocket, lost its importance as time began to run out for him. He needed shelter.

His horse had bucked him off about ten miles out of Denver City. The long and lonely walk had taken all of the strength he could muster. He placed one foot before another and had bowed his head to the cold wind of the storm.

Suddenly, he felt the strong arm of someone who

had come up in the dark. It was a young man who spoke. "Can I help you, old man?"

He snarled like a trapped dog, "Who you callin' old?"

A livery stable loomed up out of the dark in front of them and the young man helped him through the stable door. The smell that greeted them was a mixture of horses, hay, and the musty wooden barn. The wind coming through the cracks of the livery stable was stirring up the dust. The old man was taking his last steps.

The young man led him over to a couple bales of hay and then helped him to lay down. Taking a horse blanket, he covered the old man with it and lit an oil lamp for a light and what little heat it could yield.

"What's your name?" The young man asked. The old man looked the youngster over but saw only compassion in his face.

He thought, *If I had a boy, maybe this one would do.* "Henry...Henry Clay," he answered the boy with labored breath.

A ragged cough shook his body and he knew that he had shot his wad. His life was quickly coming to an end. What to do? What could he do? The map with the directions to the mine would do him no good now and there was no family to leave it to. He had traipsed around the mountains nigh on thirty years before he discovered what proved to be a rich find.

He had taken his pick axe and shovel and dug and scratched until he came across what was a lode-bearing vein. Gold is generally found throughout quartz rocks in veins sometimes called "pegmatites" or tellurium; what was commonly called gold telluride.

It had taken him seven long years of hard work, living off the land, and the occasional trips to the nearest towns to work his claim. He made a shelter in a cave and called it home. The gold had got a hold of him, and his routine never varied. Wake up, then mine the claim; back to the cave for some food, and then collapse in fatigue and exhaustion to fall asleep.

If he needed some coffee or flour and fixins for his pipe, he would head to the nearest towns or camps which were few and far between. He varied his coming and going to different settlements because he didn't want to leave a well-worn trail back to the mine.

Once a man had tried to follow him, but he was an old he-coon when it came to the woods and he lost him in the rocks near the San Miguel River. Then there were the Utes to be considered. They were the first to inhabit the Telluride Valley.

They would come in the summers and put up their tepees along the river. The headwaters of the San Miguel rose in the San Juan Mountains, southeast of the Valley. The Utes would hunt those mountains for elk, deer, and the mountain sheep high up in the range.

The river was filled with brown and rainbow trout. The char and cutthroats also called this water home, especially in the headwater area and tributaries of the San Miguel.

It was also home to the gold he had spotted in the stream and then panned it back to a rich deposit of fine flakes which some called placer gold, this led him to his discovery of a nearby vein that had been silting into the stream.

One day, he gathered up some of the "oro," as the Spanish called gold, and then started his horse for Denver City to file a claim and have the ore samples, that were tucked in his coat, assayed.

They called them Chinook winds and they are fairly common in the winter months in the Rockies. They usually blow from west to east and this here Chinook come a roarin', knocking down a lodge pole pine onto the trail.

It spooked his horse and Bessie pitched him off and then had run off with the bag of gold dust that he had painfully collected. He chuckled when he thought, *That is the richest horse in Colorado.* Coughing, he turned his eyes to the young man and told him, "I got somethin' to tell you boy."

Chapter Two

THE DIFFERENCE

He had promised the old man that he would see him get a proper funeral and burial. The parson and the undertaker were the same man. The young man who had brought Henry Clay into the livery stable had now brought his body to the town graveyard, where he stood by the grave.

The parson spoke a few words over Henry Clay and then prayed for his soul. The parson's voice echoed over the foothills as he read the twenty-third Psalm from the Bible. "The Lord is my Shepherd . . ." and then it was over.

Andy Jackson lifted his head and said, "Amen."

Andrew Jackson was the son of Hugh Jackson, a soldier from Georgia who had fought with his regiment at the Battle of New Orleans back in December 1814. Andy had listened to his father's stories into the long hours of many nights until he fell asleep.

His father idolized Andrew Jackson, no relation, but he had named his son after him. Later, when Andrew Jackson became the seventh President of the United States, there was no stopping Hugh from letting everyone know that he had fought with "Old Hickory," as his men called him.

Andy was born in 1846 and had worked with his Pa on an old, hard-scrabbled piece of land in Georgia. His mother died in 1857, and his father lost all interest in farming. Pa would join a group of his friends at the tavern, and they would talk late into the night of the West and the Rocky Mountains, and new hope for life came back in Hugh's heart.

Zebulon Pike heard a report of gold in South Park in 1807. It was near Montana City, later renamed Denver City. Prospectors had traced flakes of gold around the Platte River and along some of the creeks. Mostly, they would pan in the streams for what the Spaniards called "placer" gold. It was gold that had broken loose from the mother lode and was found in the sand of the streams due to weather and erosion.

Pa and his friends knew of a Georgia man named Lewis Ralston. He and some of his people had left for the California gold fields in a wagon train. Word was when they got out West, they had stopped near the South Platte, the other side of Montana City, in the Colorado Territory.

John Brown, who was in the wagon party, wrote in his journal, "Lay bye. Gold found." Ralston had found about an ounce of gold in his very first pan! The notation in the journal said June 22, 1850.

Every man, Jack of them, who had heard about the discovery of gold, wanted to head out. Some of Pa's friends were putting a wagon train together to go West. When they all took out, Pa felt left out cause he had a wife and son to consider. Then, when Ma died, Pa was stirred up by the stories at the tavern.

Pa had always loved a challenge, and the Western lore began to draw him there, and so with an old mule and his eleven-year-old son, Hugh set off for the Colorado Territory. They arrived at the South Platte River sometime in 1857.

Young Andy was amazed at the tents, teepees, wagons, and lean-tos that sprung up along the banks of the river. Teamsters, miners, traders, fur trappers, lumbermen, cowboys, mountain men, Indians, and dance hall girls filled the camp. They first called the settlement Montana City; later, the name was changed to Denver City after the territorial governor who had just stepped down, a James Denver by name.

The winter of '57 was tough. It seemed to Andy all he did was find and cut wood. His father hunted meat, and together, they strengthened the lean-to that they had thrown up to keep out the cold. Spring was welcomed, and 1858 saw the construction of a proper cabin.

Those were years of hard work and the beginning of a new home at the foot of the Rockies. They did not have much other than the promise of a better life. Sometimes, that is all a man has, and it keeps him going even in hard times. Pa would say, "It's only gonna get better, son."

The gold strike at Pike's Peak had lit a fire in Pa, and he lit a shuck for the promise of newfound wealth. Young Andy was left to fend for himself and did odd jobs around the town.

A woman named Thelma took a liking to him and let him ride her pony that she kept. She could make an apple pie like nobody else. She would give him a slab to eat and some cold milk from the goat she kept. Her cookin' brought hungry miners and trappers to her door. So she set up a little bakery and did a fair to middling business.

Sometimes, if she had "extry" flour, she would make a washtub full of donuts, which the men in the camp called "bear sign." They were filling, and Andy ate his share.

Time seemed to roll by, but there was no word from Pa. Andy worked a little on the cabin, making improvements to it. He landed a job at Callahan's livery stable. Callahan was an Irishman from New York City. That Irishman had been a "pugilist," as he called himself. He taught Andy how to box and hold his hands so as not to break his fingers and knuckles. He was sure big on footwork.

He taught Andy how to set your right foot for a stronger left hook and the importance of pulling back to assess your opponent's strength. The lessons in the manly art of self-defense strengthened Andy's body and mind.

Two years came and went, and it was his birthday. He had grown and was big for his age. Thelma was going to make him a birthday cake, and Callahan was invited. They were going to celebrate his birthday. It seemed as if he did not have a care in the world. He felt like the clouds that clung to the mountains just floating in the sky. Life went on. His mind did have one troubling thought: "Where is Pa, and is he alright?"

He got his answer when a trapper came to town one day and found young Andy working in the livery stable. "Your father was robbed and killed up at the

Peak!" "Who killed him?" Andy asked. "Well, boy, no one knows, but a Talbot was seen ridin' that old mule of your Pa's."

Andy sat down, and for the first time since his Ma died, he wept. Now, he would never see his Pa again. He was alone, and at fifteen, he had become a man. The West was tough, and many a youngster was hauling reins at twelve and working in the mines. It was a tough life, and they were even tougher times. You just had to make do.

It was 1861, and the gold rush at the Peak was winding down. Highwaymen with pistols began to rob and steal throughout the territory. Now, the war began to influence the inhabitants of Denver. The Southerners sang Dixie and bragged of Jeff Davis. Colorado was now officially a U.S. Territory, and the sentiments ran strong both ways.

The federal government had constructed the boundaries, taking portions of land from Nebraska, Utah, Kansas, and New Mexico. It was a shrewd move to protect the resources of gold, silver, and lead for the Union.

Then, the word went out the southern states were leaving the Union. Young Andy joined up with Colonel Slough's men and then marched down to New Mexico in 1862 on word that Confederates from Texas were headed up to destroy Fort Union. The Colonel, disobeying orders, marched his men from the fort down to Glorieta Pass in New Mexico.

The armies were about equal, and Andy was a part of the twelve hundred men that attacked the enemy. He loaded and fired his rifle until the barrel was too hot to touch. Andy found out that he was a great shot, and so did his sergeant, who then put him on the front lines to pick off the rebels.

He thought, being from Georgia, I should have joined the Confederacy, but his anger at his father's death gave way to a desire to kill. He did not care who. So he released his anger and disappointment of life into those Texicans that come flooding through the Pass. When the battle was over, they holed up at Fort Union, and then he went back to Denver City.

Upon his return, Andy found that his cabin had burned down. A fire had burned down the business district, and Pa's cabin was a rubble pile of burnt logs. General William H. Larimer had claimed- jumped the property along Cherry Creek. He took possession of the property where the cabin had stood, and Andy did not have the money to fight it nor any influence in the town that now had grown to 3,500 people. Andy thought to himself, "I will find some work and start over," never dreaming that he was about to inherit a gold mine.

Now, he stood by the side of the newly dug grave that held the remains of Henry Clay. He could feel in his pocket the parchment that was drawn by hand. There were reference points that he knew and some that he did not. One thing he did know was that he now had the difference that could change his life. He turned from the grave and strode down the hill toward town.

Chapter Three

THE CHOICE BEFORE HIM

The Colt Model 1861 Navy cap & ball .36 caliber revolver was a six-shot, single-action percussion weapon produced by Colt's Manufacturing Company from 1861 until 1873. It incorporated the "creeping" or ratchet loading lever and round barrel of the .44 caliber Army Model of 1860 but had a barrel one-half inch shorter, at seven and a half inches.

Under his raggedy Army coat, Andy had two of those Colts tucked in his belt. This represented all of his personal property, which included the rags he wore for clothes. The Denver camp was still a dangerous place to live, and Andy was no fool. He would slip out of town when he had money for powder and balls to practice drawing and shooting his pistols.

Those guns had been sold by Colt to the Navy for about twenty-three dollars each. Andy had bought his brace of pistols for thirty dollars. He had used his remaining pay when he was discharged at Fort Union. He loved the feel of those smooth walnut grips in his hand. He kept those pistols well-oiled, and the barrels were clean as a whistle. Yes, sir, not a speck of grain from the gunpowder could be seen when he was done cleaning them.

The night that he met Old Man Clay, he had been out shooting when the winter storm set in. He quickly hurried back to town and came up behind Clay, who was staggering to walk. Sensing the old man was in trouble, he grabbed ahold of him and took him to the livery where he worked for Boss Callahan.

Now that the old man was buried, he had a choice to make. He was headed back into town, and Andy ran his thoughts carefully through his mind. He had to get that gold checked out. Henry had had a small sack of nuggets in his pocket with the map. He had shown them to Andy.

Many in town thought that the assayer was dishonest. He was known to lighten the scale. He also employed a couple of head-knockers who followed and robbed prospectors who brought their gold in. He ended up with both the gold and the money he paid the miners.

Andy could file the claim, but it would cost more than he had. If he did, then that would let the cat out of the bag. He did not want a "rush" to start until he located the claim and figured out what to do with Clay's legacy, which was now his.

So, with his mind made up and knowing that the gold ore was worth something, he decided to go to the assayer's office. He was in hopes that he could get some cash so he could put together an outfit to use when he located the mine that Clay had told him about.

Andy needed tools and supplies and a horse. He knew Boss Callahan had a sorrel that was sound and could fill the bill, but he wanted too much money for it. Maybe he could strike a deal with Callahan. He just did not want to stir up trouble and have Callahan strike him. The Irishman could get a mite perturbed about money.

The teamsters were selling some of their oxen to the farmers and were getting more money for them than horses. A good horse cost about sixty dollars, and Andy just did not have it. Callahan paid him thirty dollars each month and let him sleep in the livery. He spent about two bits to eat midday. He had saved about twenty-eight dollars and put it in the bank.

Small one-hundred-acre farms were selling for about

three hundred dollars near Fremont, and he wanted to buy one and start his own ranch. There was one point where he had over two hundred dollars saved, but bandits hit the bank and cleaned it out. He started over, but if it wasn't one thing, it was another. Pa was a dreamer, and Andy was one too.

He shifted the Colts in his belt, and his brow furrowed with thought as to what he should do. What would Pa do? He needed about two hundred dollars to outfit himself for the trail. There was no getting around it; he had to take the gold ore to the assayer, get it weighed, and get as much money for it as he could.

He needed that sorrel. He would have to make a quick getaway from town once the word got out that he had gold.

Well, Bob's your uncle, it will be a time, he thought. He had made his decision, and he knew Pa would have been proud of him. He headed towards the general store and walked into trouble. A man stood at the counter and arrogantly shouted at the girl waiting on him.

She had the prettiest golden red hair a body had ever seen. The freckles on her upturned nose gave her the cutest look. She saw him staring and said, "I will be with you in a minute." He flushed, and his face felt like he was on fire. "Yes, ma'am."

He shifted his body. Andy stood about six feet tall, and his hands were like leather from the work he did at the livery stable each day. He would also soak his hands in water mixed with salt. Callahan said it would toughen the skin of his hands for boxing. He did not weigh more than 165 pounds, but he had broad shoulders and a sunburnt face. His hair was dark brown and long, and it stuck out of the bottom of his hat that, some called a cowboy hat. Its' brim was wide like a Mexican sombrero. He was awkward and shifted from one foot to the other. What a pretty girl!

The man turned and stared at him. "You'll wait til I'm done, you lil pup!" The hackles rose up on Andy's neck, and he knew that he wanted to kill this man. When he was a soldier, he did not consider himself a killer. You just did what a soldier did, and that was fight, and sometimes you killed the enemy. Andy knew that this was a dangerous man. Evil seemed to come out of this man's soul.

Andy did not like the way that he had spoken to the girl. The man finished his purchase and then turned to leave. He dropped his shoulder and knocked Andy out of his way. "Move or I'll move you, kid!"

The girl spoke up, "Mister Talbot, you forgot your change." Talbot? Could this be the man the trapper had told him about, the killer of his Pa? Talbot flung his hand at her and said, "Keep it. I'll be back to collect from you later."

The girl had tears in her eyes. Fear caused her to tremble. Andy gently said, "You don't have to be afraid; he will never hurt you. I'll see to that!" "What's your name?" she asked. "I am called Andrew Jackson," he told her.

"No, you're not!" "Yes, that's the moniker my folks gave me, but you can call me Andy." The pretty girl told him, "My name is Susan." "My father owns the store, but he left town to go to Leadville."

"Where is your mother?" Susan dropped her head and said softly, "She passed last fall." Andy felt bad for asking but quickly replied, "My Ma is gone too." He looked at this girl and knew he was in love. He had a hard time getting the words out but told her that he needed supplies for a trip.

Andy handed her his list and explained that he would pick up his supplies later. She told him that they had everything in stock and that it would cost roughly one hundred dollars. "That's a whole lot less than I thought." He told her. She promised to put the supplies together, and he informed her he would come back around five o'clock in the afternoon.

He did not see which way Talbot had gone. He knew that he needed to go to the assayers' office and then head to the bank and withdraw his money. He reached under his Army coat and put his hands around the Colts. He was ready for come what may.

No man wants to shoot another man. The Wild West had bred a tough lot. They would kill you to jump your claim. There were men who had been killed for not doffing their hat to a lady, and some were killed for cheating at cards or horse rustling. There was a code that these men lived by; it was harsh but served these lawless times.

When he walked into the assayer's office, Andy knew he was in trouble. Sitting in a chair was Talbot. "Here comes the pup!" Talbot sneered. The assayer stood and asked, "How may I help you?" Andy told him, "I need this ore assayed and would like to sell it." Andy kept his right hand free in case he had to draw down on Talbot, and with his left hand, he dumped the ore on the assayer's desk.

Talbot sat up in his chair and licked his lips with greed. He exchanged looks with Luke, as that was the assayer's name. "Well, let's see what we got," Luke said. He brought out his scale and proceeded to eyeball the ore.

He picked up a large piece that was a gold nugget. "This here weighs five ounces." Andy was not going to argue; he needed cash on the barrel head, and he needed it now. Luke informed him, "The ore is the best that I have seen!"

Luke purred like a cat over spilt milk. "Where is your mine located?" Andy knew to keep his mouth shut. "A prospector gave it to me to get assayed and cashed in," Andy said. He knew that they did not believe him. The truth was he really did not know where Clay's diggings were.

Talbot stood and pretended to stretch and then walked over to the door and checked the street. That is when Andy slid one of the Colts out and held it along his right leg. Luke's back was turned to him, and he was finishing his assay. Turning back around, he said, "This would run about three hundred dollars to the ton. The nugget is one hundred dollars, and the rest of the ore is worth about $100."

"Count it out," Andy replied. "Well, I would have to go to the bank," Luke said. "I will write you out a draft, and you can go to the bank and cash it in." The choice was before him, and Andy did not like the choice.

It was a long walk to the bank, and Talbot had a smirk on his face. Stories had gone around town of prospectors robbed and murdered when they left the office, and Talbot looked like the part of a head knocker. Callahan had told him the term head-knocker came from Five Points back in New York City.

There was a gang of Irish there who formed the Five Points gang. Callahan had lived there and told him that the district was located one block off Broadway in New York's sixth ward. A man named Paul Kelly ran the gangs of New York, and it was rumored that he was really an Italian. His head-knockers ruled the streets with violence. Talbot fit the bill.

Andy instructed them, "I'll tell you what, gather up the gold, and we will go over together, and you can help me get payment there." They did not like it one bit, no sir, not one bit. When the assayer gave Talbot a nod, Andy spotted it out of the corner of his eye. Andy brought that gun into sight, and both men froze.

"You and Talbot lead the way, and if any polecats try to jump us, then I am ready to give them a good case of lead poisoning." "Now move!" They moved! Andy let them lead the way so that he could keep them covered.

The banker eyed them as they came in. He had a twinkle in his eye. "You plan on using that weapon, young fellow?" "No sir, I am just guarding the gold we have brought over," Andy said.

Laughter in the street caused Talbot and Luke to turn red with anger. A lot of the old timers who were sitting in front of the bank had been over the mountains and back. They knew what was going on, and if not, they had a pretty good suspicion.

A couple of the boys sashayed up behind Andy to help him. They had lost their pokes to Luke and Talbot, although no one could ever prove it. Now, this young kid had "treed" both of these devils and was holding the winning hand with two Navy Colts.

The banker weighed the gold on his scale. Then he counted out two hundred and fifty dollars. That was fifty dollars more than the assayer had offered him. It was then that it dawned on Andy that he hadn't needed to go to the assayer's office. Filing a claim, yes, but getting payment for the gold could have been done right here. The problem was Talbot, and Luke now knew he had gold somewhere.

He left them stewing in their own juices and headed for the livery stable to pick up his supplies. First, he wanted that sorrel and a pack horse. Boss Callahan gave him a good deal, the sorrel, and another pack horse for one hundred dollars. He was riding high with anticipation and headed for the general store.

Susan looked more beautiful than she had earlier in the day. He was never comfortable around girls. He had no sisters and spent his years mostly around men. There were dance hall girls who were in the camp, but his Pa counseled him to give them a wide berth. So he did.

"You're back; I wondered if you would be back before five o'clock. We close around that time." The setting sun sent rays of gold into her hair. He knew that this was his girl, but how to tell her? That was the challenge.

He began to take the supplies and divide them into two packs. He did not want to place them on the pack horse until he balanced the load. He had seen some horses that were loaded improperly in the Army, and they had sores worn into their backs. He made the hitch and placed it over the pack horse. The horse turned and looked at him but did not buck or fight the hitch.

He entered back into the store and counted out the money he owed her. There was a loud voice that shouted from the street. "Hey pup, get out here. I am going to trim your hide." It was Talbot. He knew he had this to do, and a great calm came over him. He was no stranger to killing. He took his Army jacket off and laid it over the counter. He loosened both Colts in his belt and headed for the street.

A strange look came over Talbot's eyes. The man standing in front of him stood over six feet tall; his shoulders were broad, and his hands looked strong. The two Colts glistened in the setting sun. Talbot had purposely stood with his back to the sun so that it would be in the kid's eyes.

However, the kid had his hat pulled down, and Talbot could not see his eyes. Talbot would always wait until he could see fear in the eyes of his opponent. That flicker in the eyes was his edge. Talbot could not see the eyes of the kid.

Talbot wore his holsters high on his hips. Andy had practiced the cross draw and was accurate with either hand. Talbot would have to reach up to grab his gun, whereas Andy could pull across his body in one smooth motion. Many is the time that made the difference.

Suddenly, Talbot lurched forward and grabbed at his guns. He could not believe what he saw. The kid had both of the Colts in his hands, and fire spouted out of both barrels. Talbot felt something hit him in the chest. It knocked the breath out of him. His guns slid from his hands, and darkness began to cover his eyes. His last thought was, "Is the sun setting?" Talbot was dead, and as it turned out, it was his last sunset.

Susan came running out of the store. "Are you alright, Andy?" She threw herself into his arms, and for a moment, Andy was filled with a joy that he could not describe. "Yes, he will never ever bother you again." One of the old timers from the bank stood by the body and then looked up at Andy.

"Son, this was one of the brothers. There were three

Talbots. The other two will be lookin' for ye." Andy nodded and then turned to Susan and said, "I will be coming back for you." She whispered, "I will be waiting for you." He vaulted from the porch, jumped on his horse, and gave the sorrel his head. The pack horse followed. The road was before him, and the map showed the way.

Chapter Four

THE MAP

Well, as they say, Andy lit a shuck outta Denver City on that sorrel, and the pack horse did its best to follow. Denver City sits on the western edge of the Great Plains and east of the Front Range of the Rocky Mountains. The old Trapper's Trail, which was much used by the Ute peoples, led to the Continental Divide. It was nothing more than a footpath, but it had widened by the wagons and settlers pushing west during the gold rush.

The era of the mountain men had concluded by the late 1850's. The gold rush brought many wagons that were headed to the gold camps. It was greed and the lust for gold that brought these pilgrims in their wagons. They wrote in red chalk on the sides of their wagons, "Pike's Peak or Bust." There were many that went bust. They fought claim jumpers, snowstorms, starvation, and bandits, as well as roving bands of Indian warriors.

Colorado became a territory on February 28, 1861. There were two main trails that crossed the territory: the Santa Fe Trail in southern Colorado and the Overland Trail further to the north. The Overland Trail in Colorado came down from the main route, passin' through Sterling, Fort Morgan, Denver, and Fort Collins. It rejoined the main trail south of Laramie, Wyoming.

Andy was riding on the old Smoky Trail. There were some who took to calling it the Starvation Trail. The wagons and men who were rushing to the gold camps had widened it in some places. The bones of cattle, horses, and men marked this trail. Storms and blizzards trapped many who starved to death.

Andy looked back at his pack horse that carried all the food supplies he had. The bones reminded him of the danger of being unprepared. His father had taught him not to go off half-cocked but to think through his steps before deciding which way to go.

His mind was now filled with deep thoughts, and he remembered a scripture that his Pa read out of Ma's old family Bible. "But he knoweth the way that I take;

when he hath tried me, I shall come forth as gold." He had tried to find Ma's Bible in the burnt rubble sometime back, but it was gone.

What was it his Pa said? A man is more valuable than gold. Andy's struggle was the killing of Talbot but even more those that he had killed in the War. Talbot needed killing, and he got it done. He told himself that he did it for Susan's safety. Now, he would have two vengeful brothers on his trail.

He turned again to check his back trail and heard the rustling of the map in his coat. Really, he felt it more than he heard it because Clay had scrawled it on an old hide that was dried like parchment. Where he was headed was written on that hide, but he knew he would have to cover his tracks when he got off the trail.

Those brothers would be fogging the trail and coming like two bats outta hell. "Well, let 'em come." Then he bowed his head into the wind, coming down from the foothills, and plodded forward.

Chapter Five

THE GOLD IS YELLOW

It was about a three-day ride from Denver City by horse to the Front Range of the Rockies. Andy ran into many travelers headed to and from the gold camps. He spoke to none but quietly aimed his horses west.

The first night out of Denver City, he camped off the main trail. You could not be too cautious, and Andy was a very cautious man. He kept his fire to a few sticks, just enough to make coffee. Dried jerky was the only meal he allowed himself. He checked his guns, then went over into the brush away from the now extinguished fire and rolled up in his blanket.

The horses heard it first and softly snorted. That sorrel was better than a watchdog. Suddenly, Andy had those two Colts in his hand, ready for come what may.

Chief Ouray's Tabeguache was a band of Utes, but they were pretty much peaceful. Ouray had made it known that the white man could come and go into the mountains, but they were not to build houses on the land. There were a few of the Utes that were not peaceful, and the Talbots, by now, would be trailing him. Someone was coming, and Andy was ready.

◆

I held those Colts tight, and I was ready for anything. A cool night breeze brought the smell of the pines to my nose. There definitely was something out there, but what?

The bushes rustled in front of me, and there was the snap of a stick. Someone was coming. I lowered my body to make less of a target. Then I saw a head come out of the bushes. It was a fawn. It must have smelled me because it bleated and spun and jumped back into the bushes.

I waited for a little while in case someone had pushed the fawn ahead of them. The sky was graying, and I decided to pack up and go. I could hear some of the camps stirring, but I gave them a wide birth and headed out. They would cover my tracks when they started to the camps.

It took me two more days of riding before I reached

the Front Range. The map indicated that my jumping-off point was down by a creek that lay at the base of the foothills.

It was then that they came out of nowhere, and their first shot took me out of the saddle. My horse bolted, and the pack horse followed. It was the Talbot brothers, and I knew my goose was cooked.

It felt like my shoulder had taken the shot, and it was on fire. I pulled my Colts out of my belt when one of the brothers shot into my body with his pistol. I snapped off a shot at him and rolled off the trail; it was really just a footpath. The side that I chose for cover dropped off towards the stream, and that roll saved my life. I felt myself tumbling down the side, and I slid to a stop when I hit a boulder. Quickly, I crawled to the other side of the rock and waited.

No matter how careful he had been, they had tracked him and ambushed him. Now, he was in serious trouble. His anger became stronger than the pain of his bullet wounds. Well, if they wanted him, they had to come get him. Those Colts were single-action, so he cocked both triggers. One shot for each of the brothers.

My blood was on the ground where I slid. The blood was pouring from my side, so I laid one of my Colts on the rock in front of me whilst I plugged the hole in my side with my neckerchief. I could not see my shoulder as those dirty bushwhackers had shot me from behind. My head started feeling light, and I knew that I must not pass out. I had to get into that cold stream. The run-off from the snow on the mountains would make that water like ice. It would revive me.

"Do you see him?" one of the brothers yelled. "Lem, you check that side of the trail, and I am going down this side to the stream. Here he came in all of his glory. He was unshaven and had a swarthy countenance. I smelled him before I saw him. Tobacco stains were on the front of his deerskin shirt, and he was ready for action. I waited until he saw me, then I blew him away to kingdom come.

His big fat carcass rolled down the slope and landed not far from where I lay behind the rock. His face had a surprised look. He was the one who had shot me from behind. I heard his last breath go out of him.

That left me just Lem to deal with. I eased down the last three feet and slid into the water. That cold mountain stream took the pain out of my shoulder, and so I kinda drifted a few yards downstream, holding my pistols out of the water.

Lem was coming, but where and when, I did not know. Now, it was a waiting game, and I stood the chance of passing out. I never was a prayin' man, but I commenced to calling on my Maker.

My prayer was simple; I asked the Lord to let Lem come to meet Him. I was going to send Lem His way as soon as I could. As it turned out, Lem was none too bright. He had wriggled down to the water where I went in. Then he stood to take a look see which way I had gone. He looked upstream, and when he turned to look my way, both of my guns roared, and I filled him with lead, and then I passed out.

When I came to, I was staring at shiny rocks in the water next to where I had passed out. I scooped up a handful of golden yellow nuggets. I stopped and thanked the Lord for the now departed Talbots. I had struck gold after their lead struck me.

It took me some time to get back to the trail, and I fell down and passed out. The cold nose of my horse nuzzled my face, and I awoke to a brand new day. The thoughts of what had happened the previous day flooded my mind. The pain in my back and side reminded me that I had been shot.

I knew that I had to move. There was a box of matches in my saddle bags, so I slowly pulled myself up by the stirrup. The horse must have smelled my blood and started to act up. "Whoa, boy, whoa." I got the matches, then just fell down.

When I came to, the fire was blazing, and my blanket covered me. My head was resting in my saddle, and the oldest-looking man I ever saw was watching me with two brown hawk-like eyes. He said, "Howdy boy, I borrowed some of your coffee, and it is mighty tasty."

"You'se some shot up! I got the bullet out of your shoulder. The other hole in your side the bullet went through. I have been watching ya nigh onto a week." A week, he had said. I had been unconscious for a week?!

I certainly appreciated what the old man had done to save me, but who was he? He must have read my mind. He spoke what I was a-thinkin'. "I am an old trapper, but the gold rush has ruined my trade. Not many of us mountain men left. I was here before Bridger or Carson."

Everyone knew who Bridger was. James Felix Bridger was an early mountain man, trapper, and an Army scout. He was still kicking around the West and was in his fifties. This old timer must be in his sixties, I thought.

"Ya a hunting for gold?" When he said that, I remembered the nuggets I found before I passed out. He laughed, "I found them nuggets in your hand when I stumbled on ya. They're fool's gold, iron pyrite; ya got a handful of nothing but shiny rocks. Howsomever, that map looks promising."

I put my hand in my shirt and discovered the map was gone! When I looked up at him, he was holding the map in his hand. "Ya lookin' for this?" He tossed it over to me. Then he stood and bent over the fire, poured a cup of coffee, and brought it over to me. I drank it and watched him. I must have drifted off into a deep sleep because the next morning when I woke up, he was gone!

Rolling over, I took a quick look-see around the perimeter of the camp. A habit I picked up from my Army days. A man can't be too careful. The horses were both tied to a picket line between two shrub bushes. My packs were on the ground, and one looked a little lighter.

Well, bless him for saving my life. My thoughts immediately went to how fortunate I had been: Henry Clay's map and nuggets, the banker's giving me the cash, the shoot-out with Talbot, and the lovely Susan. She kinda took the sting out of my brush with death.

There was the showdown at the creek and an old trapper that just happened to come along in the nick of time. Some called it Providence, but it makes a body wonder if there really is a God. Well, if so, He certainly was lookin' after me.

I rustled out of that camp, and I began to think about God and what some called Providence. It seemed that everything, whether good or bad, was called God's will. I just could never bring myself to believe that.

I can still hear my father's gravel voice sayin', "God gets blamed for things He nary did! Why some of them preachers would have you believe that He is behind every evil thing." Ha! Pa was a ripsnorter when he got started.

When Ma died, Pa stopped the preacher from talking at the funeral. The minister said, "God took our dear sister in His sovereign will." Pa jumped up and said, "Consumption took her life!" Then Pa quoted James 1:17 back to the minister, "Every good gift and every perfect gift is from above. Sickness is not good, so it did not come from God!"

Whew! It was all over but the shouting. That was the last time that Pa ever darkened the door of a church. When the undertaker asked Pa what he wanted for words on the stone, Pa told him, "God is always good!" Then I heard him say, "Let the preacher study at that." Well, I whispered a prayer, thanked the good Lord for sparing my life, and headed out.

Chapter Six

OVER THE RIVER & THROUGH THE WOODS

There is a small tributary that flows at the base of the Front Range. It eventually flows down to the Platte. The base of the foothills has dense growth, and there are many kinds of trees.

I saw a cluster of quaking aspen along the river banks. There was a line of pines going up the grade. You had your lodge pole pine mixed with ponderosa pine; then, as I crossed back over the stream in the shallows, you had your cottonwoods growing right on the banks of the stream. It was sure beautiful.

It was getting downright chilly. I had forgotten my old Army coat at the store. When I took it off to go out and fight Talbot, I laid it over the counter. Thankfully, one of the things that I purchased was a buckskin coat.

So I dug it out of one of the packs and put it on.

It grew colder the further up I rode, and I knew that higher up was some Douglas fir and blue spruce. An eagle was twirlin' around in the sky, and I saw a hawk a watchin' me from his perch in a cottonwood. I kept a sharp lookout as I rode through the woods.

Although Chief Ouray had promised peace, there were a few renegades that kinda did what they wanted. The Utes, along with many of the plains Indians, were noble warriors and a proud people. The white man had lied to them and broke treaty after treaty.

It was then my pack horse sorta screamed, or so it seemed to me. When I turned around, two arrows were stuck in her side. I didn't see where the arrows came from, and I didn't see those Utes until they were right on top of me!

They were on me in a moment's time, and I didn't even have a chance to pull my guns. There were two warriors that I could see, and they were some fierce. The Plains Indians were a noble race. They were very skilled horsemen and had a strength that some white men did not have. The Utes were strengthened by the land and the mountains, which bred some tough braves.

A man loses his strength or, in some cases, never gains it when he lets others do things for him. I have learned to only rely on myself. That is how I survived on my lonesome back in the camp.

It looked like these were probably some of the renegades that had broken off from Ouray. I reacted out of self-preservation. The first warrior took me off my horse, and I landed on that wounded shoulder; before I could roll over, he was on me, and the second was coming up quick. He swung a club at my head, and I rolled out of the way, picked up a rock, and struck him in the head. The other warrior was lithe and supple, and he could fight. The problem was he had a knife, and I had my two pistols.

Call it luck or Providence, I caught him in the temple with the butt of my Colt, and down he went. I am no murderer. Whilst he was examining the back of his eyelids, cause I knocked him out cold, I grabbed hold of them and tied their hands with my piggin strings. I still had them from when I cowboyed, and we would use them to tie down the cattle for branding.

When I stood up and turned around, there was a line of Ute warriors that rode out of the trees, and they were led by Chief Ouray! I had seen him at Fort Collins once. So I just laid down my guns and raised my hands. I prayed my goose wasn't cooked.

He motioned to me and made signs that he wanted to palaver. The old scouts would sit down and talk with the Indians using hand signs and a smattering of words to communicate. Old Bridger called it palavering.

The great chief hisself climbed down, spread a blanket, and motioned to me to approach. Yes, sir, and I did. The story was that Ouray had worked as an indentured servant in Taos, New Mexico, and there he learned to speak Spanish and some English even before he learned the Ute and Apache languages, which was sometime later in his life.

I had heard he was called the white man's friend, and I was praying that he was my friend. He started by making a motion with his hands. He came for a peace talk. Whew! I was glad to see that. Then he pointed to one of the braves I had tied up.

He spoke, "Son." That brave warrior was his son! Next, he made a sign of a bird flying and pointed to the rippling stream and the waving grass nearby. I understood He was making some kind of an agreement with me. Near as I could figure out because I spared his son, so he was sparing me as long as the birds fly and the stream flows and the grass grows. I knew that this was big medicine.

Then he pointed at me and spoke, "Son." Whew, I was relieved! He adopted me into his tribe that day, and I was his son. Turning to all of the braves, he pointed at me and spoke again, "Son." That was it. He got up, folded the blanket, climbed on his horse, and left with his braves.

The one brave, who was not his son, looked back at me, and I knew he wanted to kill me. I had shamed him in front of his people, but could I help it that he couldn't defend himself? After all, he started the fracas, not me. I was just minding my business and enjoying the scenery when he killed my pack horse, and I was partial to her.

The trappers used to cache their supplies if they could not carry them all on their journey. They would strategically place them where they went into the woods and then reserve them for their return trip back to civilization.

Sometimes, they would build cairns out of rocks, putting the supplies in the ground and building rocks on top of the hole. Howsomever, it didn't always work as the bears would smell out the food, knock the rocks over, dig down, and get into the food.

Others would build small hut-like structures up in the trees and cache their supplies in them. Bears climbed trees and squirrels, too. Sometimes, it would work. I knew that I could not carry all of my supplies on my horse, so I had to cache some of them here.

I saw a stand of lodge pines nearby and knew that

the tribes used them to make teepees. My thought was to cut down four long poles and build a small tower. So, using my axe, I went to work. Then, I dug four holes in the ground and put poles several feet down into the dirt. I piled rocks at the base of each pole and then shimmed up and tied four crosspieces to each pole using my piggin strings. The two braves didn't need them anymore, but I did.

I didn't bury the pack horse, figuring that the animals would get their fill eating her and leave my supplies alone. I laid several limbs across the cross pieces, and I had my platform about ten feet in the air. I hauled that canvas bag from the horse. What to leave and what to take?

During the last couple of miles, I spotted the granite rock that was on the map. It had a face like a man. The nose was sticking out above the river as if it was a smellin' the water and pines.

I figured I would have a half a day's ride into the woods before I came upon the granite face. Then, depending on how long it would take me to find the next landmark leading to Clay's old diggings, I figured for three days in, three days out, and a week at the mine. Near as I could figure, I was headed south by southwest, maybe. It is easy to get turned around, and the West is so vast, and the distances can be deceiving.

One time, I went fishing in a mountain lake north of Denver City. I hooked a trout and stepped down to grab it and haul it out. The next thing I knew, I was over my head, and I lost the pole with the fish still hooked on it. That water was so clear that what I thought was only a couple of feet deep proved to be over my head!

My guess was that it would take me about half a month. So I took about a pound of coffee and flour. There was some fat back wrapped in a muslin cloth and some salt and beef jerky. I took matches and several candles for the mining and a pick axe and my axe, caps, balls, and powder for my two Colts. I put the rest of the supplies into the canvas bag and then hauled it up by rope to the top of the platform.

I tied it off at the top of the bag and rolled it over so that the birds couldn't get at it. I knew when I got into the woods that I would have to blaze a trail that I could follow out when I was done at the mine. I had come up the Starvation Trail and briefly the Overland Trail, but this was a new trail, and it was a trail to nowhere.

I put together my "possibles" bag and "soogan" to travel with. My possibles bag had a beaver tail leather flap. It carried my matches, candles, jerky, caps, balls, powder, and tin coffee cup. I had learned to travel with a soogan in the Army. Down in Old Mexico, the vaqueros used them, and we 'uns in the Army learnt it from them.

You take a quilt or wool blanket, then wrap it in a waterproof slicker or tarp. I always carried a Spanish blanket and put my gear and food in it and wrapped it, then tied it off and fitted it in behind my saddle. We called it a soogan leastways the Mex vaqueros did.

I was beat to a fare thee well. The work had taken me all day to complete. I sorted my possibles and soogan by the light of a small fire; just a cupful of fire. I wasn't taking any chances with my hair. There was still one brave who would love to take it, and I wasn't in a scalping mood. So I just laid down on the ground and put my head on the saddle and wrapped in my blanket, and the stars disappeared.

Chapter Seven

GRANITE ROCK WITH THE FACE OF A MAN

The last vestiges of winter clung to the land, and a cool breeze brought me to my senses quick. I moved that sorrel into the trees, and the cover kept most of the snow from slowing me down. It was slick along the stream, and the rocks were still covered with ice.

I worked the tree line up the creek and moved deeper into the woods when downed trees or rocks blocked my path. I figured I would be at the granite face around midday.

There have been many a philosopher born in a saddle. My thoughts were running downhill, and I shook my head to clear my mind. The constant peril that I had lived with since I helped Henry Clay had kept me on edge. My journey this day brought a ray of hope to my soul.

I counted my blessings as my Ma had taught me. My body was gaining strength by the day; there was a good horse under me, and my prospects were looking up. The map promised wealth and a certain young girl promised . . . well, I couldn't let my imagination get loose, but she was in my thoughts more and more each day.

Henry Clay spent his whole life working and prospecting to die. Life had to have a greater meaning and purpose than that. What did I have? My horse, a map, and a girl, and how did I know that she was still waiting?

So I kept riding my horse and scouting the right bank of the stream whilst pondering life as I knew it. One thing was for sure: I had to find that mine if things were to get better for me.

I almost missed it! The stream veered away from the ridge into the woods, right where the granite face was. I had been riding the left bank and keeping from the ice and rocks. When I lifted my eyes to check where the sun stood in the sky, I saw the face of the man in the rock.

I came off that horse and stood a-staring. The map said there was a bear tree; I figured Clay meant a tree that a bear had clawed. Bearclaw Johnson was an old mountain man from way back. Once, he come by our cabin and told me and Pa that the grizzlies marked the trees to set their territory and also to attract the females.

I was looking for such when I saw the carving, and that was what I was staring at. Old man Clay had carved a figure of a bear with an arrow under it. I began to walk the way the arrow indicated when I saw up ahead another arrow. I knew that Clay had blazed a trail!

Leading the sorrel, we walked deeper into the woods and found another blaze. My heart was racing with excitement. I pulled out the parchment and saw a line from the bear tree. That old man had blazed a trail to nowhere, which now became the trail to gold.

The blaze marks came to an end. So I looked at the map. I squatted down on my heels, and that is what saved me. A bullet whapped into the tree next to me, and I heard cursing. Someone was ahead of me in the bushes.

The Talbots were dead, and the only enemy I could think of was that brave that I had walloped. He sure looked like he was coming back to get me someday. The cursing was in English, so that left the Ute out.

"Jackson! Throw down your guns!" Now, that was a familiar voice. He knew my name. My mind searched my past, but it came up empty. I gripped my pistols tighter. They appeared in my hand when the bullet struck the tree.

I had spent the fall and winter practicing the "fast draw" that I had heard about in Denver City. When I confronted the first Talbot in the street in Denver City, that practice paid off.

A cook at the Four Mile House first told me about a fast draw kid; then, a trooper that I was stationed with at Fort Collins told me about a gang of desperados ridin' out of Texas. Their leader was known for getting his pistol in action quicker than anyone had ever seen.

His name was Cullen Baker, and he could drag those Colt Dragoons out and go to town like nobody's business. He came a roarin' out of Tennessee with his bunch of desperados. They shot up Union soldiers and citizens in Texas, Arkansas, and Louisiana. He was about eleven years older than me, and I first heard about him in Denver and then again when I was stationed at Fort Union.

I never had met him yet, but I sure enough done heard about him. So there I crouched, waiting for my attacker to reveal himself. Whoever he was, he knew my name and wanted me at his mercy, which I would be if I dropped my guns.

My jaw dropped when I saw who it was!

Chapter Eight

THE CURLY WOLF

We had an old wolf that came around the cabin. Pa and I took to leaving scraps out for him, and we didn't even have much for ourselves. That wolf was gaunt, and his ribs showed. Tough winter all around for all of us that year. There was an expression some of the men used if you were bold or fearless; they called such a one a "curly wolf."

Well, we had a real curly wolf that took a chance to come around to find something to eat. Pa said, "Be careful. If he feels good enough, he might bite the hand that feeds him." That wolf took a liking to me, and I treated him like you would a dog. I made him a leather collar loose enough so as not to choke when he got bigger. Sometimes, I would look around, and he would follow me from a distance.

The funny thing was when Pa left, that ole wolf disappeared! Well, neighbor, standing in front of me was a curly wolf, but it was a man. It was the old mountain man who had tended me. He had dug my bullets out and built a fire to warm me and just watched over me in general. Now, I was staring down the business end of a fifty-caliber rifle. He had the drop on me, so I gently laid those Colts down, stood up real slow, and moved back.

"Ya surprised to see me, ain't you?" I realized right then that he had memorized the map or even made a copy. Leastways, I was still breathing, and he was still talking. He also held all the aces in that fifty caliber that looked at me with its one eye.

I started to slow boil. I never had me a quick temper, and it took a lot to rile me up. The anger in me made me as mad as a wet hen. Why had he not kilt me? Why was he standing there smirking? Then it dawned on me he had not figured out the last clue, so for him, it was still the trail to nowhere. Ha! I had him over a barrel, and he knew it.

He needed me in case the old man had given me the final clue. He had missed me on purpose. The truth was Clay had told me one thing that he had not written down on the map. So nonchalantly, I strolled over, picked up my Colts, and shoved them in my waist. I said to him, "Coffee?" He put the rifle down.

I grabbed my possibles bag from the sorrel and got out the fixins for coffee. He produced a coffee pot, which I didn't have. My canteen had been filled up from the mountain stream from the morning, so I poured it in the pot and threw in a generous handful of coffee. He built a fire, and in no time, we had a pot boiling.

Well, it was time to palaver again. I spread my soogan on the ground, and we sat down. The old man began to speak when the arrow took him in the throat! That Ute brave let out a yell, and he and I were at it. I knew he would come back, and he had with a vengeance. The last time he looked back when he rode away with Chief Ouray and his warriors, I saw it in his eyes.

He had indianed up on us whilst we were fixin' to talk. He came out of nowhere, loosing that arrow as his calling card. Now, nobody was home as that old mountain man left this "mortal coil," as the English bard said. I read it in one of Miss Thelma's books. She had helped me to read better.

Now, neighbor, I was just done with it. The constant peril that I had lived with finally boiled over, and that Ute was dispatched to the happy hunting ground. My guns flashed fire, and that brave warrior died. There were some who said that the only good Indian is a dead one. I strongly disagreed.

The Federal government had signed a treaty with the Cheyenne and Arapaho when they organized the Colorado Territory. It was right before the South had fired on Fort Sumter.

Then, treaties were broken, and the lies of politicians went against these noble warriors. They fought to defend their homes and land. Just like you and I would to protect our homes and loved ones.

Ouray was a peaceful man. He desired peace. When his son and this brave warrior attacked me, I did not kill them out of respect. Now, this brave had to count coup or bring my hair back to the lodges to regain respect, and Ouray and his braves lived by that code.

Maybe you wonder why I did not give him a chance. Fight with him hand to hand and wrestle til one of us died. The truth was I had given him a chance the first go-round. He came asking for it again, and I obliged him. That was the code he and I shared, a mutual respect. He died in battle and now would be honored by his people.

It took me the rest of the day to dig their graves and bury them. My Lord, I was petered out. I had drunk the coffee, collected my new coffee pot, unsaddled my horse, picketed him, and made up my bed. It was a really nice meadow that caught the dying rays of the sun.

The soogan was spread, and I put the oilskin slicker on the ground to keep dry from the night dew. The blanket was on top with the saddle as my pillow. I pulled my boots off and stirred the fire. Then I went to sleep.

Chapter Nine

BEHIND THE SPLIT ROCK

That night in Callahan's livery stable, Henry Clay talked between coughing and gasping for breath; he knew his time was up. I had listened closely to every word and looked at the map he had carried in the sputtering light of the lamp that I had lit.

I tried to make him comfortable there in the hay. He started to doze off, and then some inner energy would bring new life and strength to him. He motioned me closer and said, "The split rock at the end of the trail. It looks like it is done, and there is nowhere to go, but it is in the split rock..."

I guess you could say I named it the Trail to Nowhere. That night, my journey began on that trail to nowhere. Ma was dead; Pa was gone. I had twenty-eight dollars to my name and no future. My cabin was burned down, and a powerful, rich man had laid claim to our land. I was nobody.

There was a fancy lodging place called the Four Mile House in Denver City. They had started construction back two years before, in 1859, about the same time me and Pa began our cabin. When I came into the territory with Pa, there were a bunch of shacks and teepees down along the Platte.

It was called Montana City then, but now it was Denver City, and it was a-changing. In the early 1800s, settlers began moving into the Colorado Territory, mostly fur traders and trappers, in 1821.

The Ole Santé Fe Trail opened up between the Missouri brakes and New Mexico and crossed through the southeastern portion of Colorado. The Spanish had settled in the territory around 1598. The oldest town in the Territory was in the San Luis Valley. San Luis was founded in the year of our Lord, 1852. There was also a small settlement at Fort Pueblo that started in 1842, ten years earlier.

Trails brought new settlers, new hopes and new dreams, and the promise of something better. I was on this trail to nowhere, wanting all these things, too. I had nothing. The end of this trail promised something.

I had traveled a bit traipsing around that country when I joined Colonel Slough when we escorted an Army train from Fort Union to Fort Pueblo. We had run into a bunch of Cheyenne warriors, and the fight was fierce and was over before you knew it. They came at us quick and disappeared just as fast. Sometimes, those war parties would test your strength, and then they were gone.

The cook at the Four Mile House was a Frenchie, and he could cuss in three languages. He would come over to Pa's and my cabin, and he was the one that had told me about Baker lately of Texas and his fast drawing. I guess it was a challenge to my boyish pride, but I determined that night I would be faster. That French man's story probably saved my life. What if I had never practiced with those pistols? Then, I would have never met Henry Clay that winter night.

Well, I have learnt that ya can't have too many what-ifs, but one thing I did have was the map with the trail to nowhere on it and the whispered last words of Henry Clay that contained the final clue to the gold.

I awoke to a new morning. I had come to the end of my trail to nowhere. When I stood up and stretched, I saw the split rock face at the end of the meadow. I took off without a how do you do and headed to the rock.

Later, I figured out that I was in what was known as

the Telluride Valley. The Utes used it to stock up and rest in the summers. I was south of Denver City and a long way from a beautiful girl with golden red hair. Her last words gave me hope, "I will be waiting for you."

I saw a flash of gray out of my right eye. When I spun to look, it disappeared into the trees. It looked like a wolf. So I kept my eyes peeled. Who knew where the nearest settlement or body was? I learnt that you had to depend on your own self if you were to make it.

Pa was gone, and Ma as well. There were those who helped me, like Miss Thelma or Callahan, but I had learnt to carry my own weight. The thought of the Providence of God came into my mind, so just to cover my bets, I tipped my hat to Heaven and headed towards the rock face.

How many times had I wondered if I would ever see my folks again? I wanted to believe in God and that there was a Heaven, but it was hard for me to come to grips with the reality of both.

A stream flowed at the base of the rock face. I saw flecks of gold and knew that it was not "fool's gold." When I walked along the rock face, I saw an indentation that jutted out from the main formation. The closer I got, the more it was, just as Clay had told me: there was a crevice that hid a small opening behind it. The trail to nowhere started here.

Wedging myself into the crevice, I saw that there was a small chamber with just enough room for me to turn around. Candles and rope lay on the chamber floor. There was a sinkhole in the chamber floor, and it had candle wax that had dripped around the rim.

I lit a candle and leaned over to see how far down it was. It looked like there was a shovel lying on the ground beneath. It could not have been ten feet to the bottom. How could I get down and, more importantly, get back up? Looking around the chamber, I saw that under the rope was a wooden beam. That old man had made do.

I took the wooden beam and laid it across the hole with a couple of feet on each side. The rope was tied to the center of the beam. Here was my way in and out. I set the beam in place, lowered the rope down, and went down hand over hand.

I relit the candle and saw there was a tunnel eroded by water over time. There are many types of caves, and water can cause erosion, forming sinkholes and subterranean passages. It seemed this formation was limestone, and I saw the blaze mark on the wall. It was the bear with the arrow underneath!

God bless that old man. I started down the passage, and when it turned a corner, I came into a cave and stepped out into that glorious sunlight. Stretching before me was a little park with trees and a small grassy flat. I immediately saw the diggings and a mine entrance . . . the Clay mine!!

I could tell that Clay had cut down trees to make the wooden mine supports as he followed the vein into the side of the hill. Quartz lay on the ground where he had crushed it to separate the gold from the quartz. There was smoky quartz and rose quartz lying in pieces on the floor of the mine entrance. What looked like chalcedony as well? Those miners who came to eat Thelma's pies and donuts were good teachers, and I remembered these different kinds of rock.

Henry had a cot and utensils in the front part of the mine and must have lived in the mine. I knew he had lived in the mouth of the cave at first because I saw the old fires and their smoke that was left on the top of the cave. The time must have come when he moved into the mine.

Then, my heart began to beat fast. Lying along the wall of the mine were bags made out of deerskins. My eyes were now accustomed to the darkness of the shaft, and there were at least twenty bags filled with gold nuggets and dust. I wished my pa could have been here to share in my joy at this newfound wealth. I was rich and had need of nothing.

I would take these back first and get me the money I needed to operate and, more importantly, marry a certain girl who was awaiting me. The long job of carrying the gold out of the underground passage awaited me, and later, taking the additional diggings out the same way would prove to be a daunting task.

Grabbing a bag in each hand, I staggered with the weight of the gold to the entrance of the shaft. Whew! The sunlight hit my face head-on, and it must have hit my brain, too. When I came out of the shaft, I saw where Henry had tied his horse and a little corral tucked over against the cave where I had come out.

How in Sam Hill had he got that horse here? It didn't come through that underground passage nor down the hole, and he could not have got it through the crevice in the split-face rock. There must be another way in and, for that matter, out!

Where was the other entrance? The sound of the waterfall was calming to my mind, so I sauntered over to the small pool it formed and sat down to think. My eyes covered this small park, which had been hidden for perhaps centuries. Maybe since the Good Lord made creation. One thing for certain: that horse did not fly in here.

I looked towards the cave that led to the underground passage. Was there a fork in the cavern that gave another access to the park? I had missed seeing the little corral Henry had made next to the entrance to the cave. What else was I missing? Then I turned my eyes to the left side of the rock face that climbed straight up almost two hundred feet or more. There was no way that Henry lowered a horse down that way with ropes.

The side opposite the cave was the mine. I would go in and explore it for a possible exit. I looked at that falling water and wondered where this water was goin'. The pool must be going into a sinkhole because there was no stream running from the pool.

When I came into the Telluride Valley, there was a waterfall up a box canyon. I had tethered my horse near there this morning before I came in. I needed to get movin'. My horse needed me, and I needed him. I decided then and there to take one bag out and get back to Denver City. My sorrel could not carry the weight of those twenty bags, and I was hard-pressed to carry two bags.

I took one last look at the falls and rose to leave when I saw that wolf again. He ducked behind the falls and disappeared. I walked over to investigate. There had to be a way out behind the falls! Thank you, Mr. Wolf. Quickly, I went around the pool and came up the side of the falls. There was a horse's hoof print in the mud!

I eased up to the falling water and saw a path going behind the falls. Walking slowly now, because I did not want to slip, I went behind the falling water. There was an entrance behind the falls, and a ray of sunshine shone at the back of that passage.

I walked towards the light. My deliverance was nigh. The walls of that park could not hold me in nor keep me from my future. Hallelujah! I laughed, realizing that I sounded like them Bible thumpers that shouted under that old canvas tent that had come to Denver City last year. I even danced a jig like they did when they got happy.

If'n I got religion, it would have to be a joyful experience for me. I kinda felt like Pa when he put on Ma's tombstone; God is always good! A good God will make you happy. I sure enough cut me a step.

I carefully made my way along a cut that led to a box canyon. When I came to the entrance to that canyon, I could see the valley before me. Off in the distance, I saw my sorrel. Now, I was going home!

Chapter Ten
THE TRAIL TO HOME

That sorrel needed a name. Pa used to call that old mule of his Lazarus. He said the mule walked like he had just rose up from the grave. It was the slowest critter we ever had. Yet it had made the long trek from Georgia to Colorado slow and steady but dependable.

I stroked that horse's muzzle, and he turned his head to me. We were pals. He had been with me from that livery stable in Denver City to this Valley. He had come to me when I was lying on the trail and touched my face.

A horse's muzzle is very sensitive. His whiskers help him to sense things close to his nose, and the skin is almost hairless. Pa said if you take care of your animals, they will take care of you.

Well, sir, that horse had sure stuck with me. He was

like my guardian angel. He . . . wait, that was it, Angel! I would call him Angel. I tore up a handful of grass and beckoned to him with it.

"Here Angel! Here, boy." He lifted his head and looked at me, and then he took a step towards me. Oh boy, my horse had a name, and I had a friend.

Taking the tether off his feet, we headed back to the box canyon that came out into the Valley. I knew that the Utes didn't come around until summer, and the cold wind sweeping the valley floor reminded me winter was a-hanging on for a few more weeks. It was getting cold again.

Well, it was all or nothing. We winded back along the passage to the entrance to the park and waterfall. Angel was as sure-footed as you would expect from a cutting horse. He could turn on a dime. When Callahan bought him from a broke cowboy, that fellow took off running at a full-speed gallop and then stopped the horse so quick that its hind quarters came up in the air. Then he ran it full speed between two barrels behind the livery stable and weaved in and out with nary an inch between the horse and the barrels.

A cutting horse will work with his rider. This gives the cowboy a partner in handling cattle. When ridin' herd, a good cutting horse will keep the cattle moving and stop a steer from taking a detour. It was worth its weight in gold. That expression was exactly what Angel was to me now.

We came out from behind the falls into the park, and I led Angel to the makeshift corral that Henry had made out of branches and brush. There was some dry grass that stood in a bunch in the middle of that park, so I took my knife and cut a pile for Angel to eat.

We were stayin' the night, and I was plumb tired from the day. Tomorrow, we were heading home. The fire that was now built gave off an eerie glow against the night that came down like a black curtain. Its warmth made a body feel good, and it stood as a sentinel against the cold night. I fell asleep.

Angel snorted, and I came up out of my blanket like a jackrabbit, guns in both hands. The day had busted, and the sun was shining. What was troubling my horse? Then I saw him again, it was that wolf. Well, I put my guns back in my belt and let him go. He had shown me the way out.

Now, I began to think about the way in. If I was to get the gold out in the future, then I needed to scout a trail going back so as I could bring me a wagon and team of horses back to carry the gold out. I could build a shack up in the box canyon to stock with supplies. I knew the Utes would be coming into the Valley come summer, so maybe Ouray would allow me to stay as I was now his adopted son.

The passage into the falls could be enlarged, and maybe I could lay down a few rails and get me a mule to pull a rail cart back and forth. My mind was swirling with plans. I rubbed Angel down with a handful of grass as I did not have me a curry brush. Then, I threw it down for him to eat it. Then I rustled me up some grub. That new coffee pot was the last thing the old mountain man had shared with me. Now it was mine.

That Ute brave probably did me a favor when he kilt that old man. We were headed for a showdown, and I did not want to kill that old man, but gold can do strange things to a man's mind. Well, at least I had me a coffee pot to remember him by.

Taking the few remaining supplies, which went into my sack, I began to pack up. Angel lifted his head, and you could tell he was ready to go as well. Well, we headed out, under the falls, through the passage, and out into the box canyon, where the sunshine hit my face; even Angel had a spring in his gait. We were headed home.

A wagon would have no problem from the box canyon to the entrance to the Valley; its floor was flat and dry. The snow that remained highlighted the rocks and bushes, but it would be no problem bringing a team into the mine.

A blur flashed across the corner of my eye. It was that gray wolf following along with us. Well, let him come. There was a feeling of satisfaction that was in me, but I also kept feeling a brooding like a dark cloud over my head. Worry is a terrible thing. Someone had once told me that it is the interest on the trouble that never comes. There is always a brighter day when the storm passes by, and the sun shines again.

My cache was back along the San Miguel River. But there was a stretch coming out of the Valley that looked to the north. I decided to leave my supplies cache right where they were and scout this new way towards Denver City.

I knew that there was a small trail that wound down toward the foothills south of Denver City. Most of the trails followed along the course of rivers and streams. The Telluride Valley was southwest of Denver City. There were no rivers that connected the two places. You had to traipse around God's creation to get back. I knew that the Uncompahgre summit lay to the east, and Sheep's Mountain was just north of that range.

I planned on heading towards Leadville, where Susan's father had gone, and I'd pick up the Starvation Trail on the other side of Pike's Peak. There were a couple of passes that could take me through the mountains, but they were probably still snowed in.

There was Owl Creek Pass that was high up. No matter how you cut it, I would have to go through one of the passes. Getting a wagon through coming back meant late spring. The summer would be no problem. I also considered going west and following the San Miguel River to the Colorado River, but the Colorado River was impassable in certain spots, and it ran through many deep canyons.

Then, there was an old warrior path that began somewhere near Sheep Mountain. The Utes had found a pass that was grassy and easily manageable. It wasn't as high up as Owl Creek Pass, and perhaps the snow was not as deep as the higher elevations. The other side went to Pike's Peak and the Starvation Trail. I pointed my horse north and started off.

Angel must have sensed my excitement at getting home cause I had to rein him back a mite as he was wanting to trot. A cool head and hands were needed now. I figured that I had enough supplies to get back. That is why I didn't go back to my cache. I hadn't planned on the gold stored in the bags waiting for me.

There would have been food for a week to last me whilst I dug gold. So, I was confident that my supplies were enough to get me home. I had lived for years on not enough. Now, it seemed that I had just enough to get me back. When I cashed in this gold dust and nuggets, I would have more than enough!

The days on the trail to nowhere had taken their toll on my body and mind. The perils of the brothers coming after me, the shoot out, being wounded, the attack of the two warriors, and the confrontation with the old mountain man made me wish for better days; like Pa's words, "It's only going to get better son," had proven to be prophetic.

When Ma would read to him from the Bible, Andy had pictured the Old Testament prophets lookin' like Pa. Hugh was a tall, gaunt man with long gray hair and a flowing beard to match. His Ma had nicknamed her husband "Moses," and that would always get a laugh from Pa. They didn't have much, but they had each other.

Those days going home on the trail gave me strength the farther that I rode. What was my future to hold? I had money or at least the gold to get it. I figured I had about Five thousand dollars in the bag. That was fourteen years of money compared to what I had been making at Boss Callahan's livery stable!

I had dreamed of a ranch near Fremont. It hit me that I now had the money to buy it! I would stock it with a small breeding herd to get started and get me a prize bull to do it with. I picture the layout in my mind, and before you know it, I was at the Starvation Trail.

Chapter Eleven

THE FIGHT FOR HOPE

There she was, Denver City, and it looked like it had grown a mite. I turned my horse towards the livery stable and was surprised when a man I did not know came out when I went to stable my horse.

"Where's Callahan?" I asked him. His answer pole-axed me, "He sloped with that widow Thelma, and every man is angry about it. She made the best pies and donuts in Denver." "Well, I am Andy Jackson, and I used to work here."

"Yep, ole Callahan told me you would be coming," he responded.

"I want to put my horse up and store my things if you don't mind. Rub my horse down and give him some oats, please, and I'll settle up with you later," I told him.

The stableman's name was Herman, and he had come over from Germany to find his fortune, which right now was shoveling manure and cleaning the stalls. We all got to start somewhere. I had learnt that where you start is not where you are going to finish.

Andy wanted to run to the store to see Susan. He grabbed his bag of gold and headed as quickly as he could to the store. A bespectacled man met him when he walked in. It was Susan's father. As soon as he saw me, he knew me. "You must be Andrew Jackson?"

"Yes, sir." I was as polite as could be as I wanted to make a good impression on Susan's father. When I started looking around the store for her, he chuckled and said, "She went out with Luke, the assayer, for a picnic."

My heart sank into my boots. What was this? She had told me that she would be waiting for me. That foreboding feeling hit me right then and then, and a jealousy came up on the inside of me. I was ready to go to war!

"He picked her up in a buckboard and headed to the creek for a picnic near where you and your Pa built that cabin."

"Thank you," I replied and then bolted out the door back to the livery stable. Angel had not been unsaddled, so I forked that horse and headed in a full gallop to Cherry Creek. I checked my guns as I rode.

Those miles flew by under the feet of my horse. There would be a reckoning! Luke was going to get weighed and found wanting in the balances. That was a scripture Ma read to me, and now I was going to read to him from the book.

I heard the scream before I saw them. Luke had her pinned down under a tree and was trying to force himself on her. When Luke saw me, he jumped up and dragged Susan towards the stream. He pulled a knife and laid it under her chin and across her throat. "Hold it, Jackson, right there!"

"I will kill her if you get any closer!" When I looked into Susan's eyes, I saw something that stirred my heart; it was the look of love. I thought, "What in blue blazes was she doing here with this polecat?"

It all happened so fast that it was over in a minute. A gray blur came out of nowhere and grabbed Luke's arm. It was that curly wolf. When the wolf attacked, Susan fell and rolled free. Luke's assaying days were over, and I was going to fill him full of lead when Susan cried out, "Don't, Andy, don't kill him!"

When the wolf turned loose, I cut loose and hit Luke smack dab in the jaw. There were two hits that day. I hit Luke, and he hit the ground. It was over. Then I took Susan in my arms, and we held each other tight. She was soft to the touch, and my heart was filled up with joy. This was my woman.

I tied Angel to the back of the buckboard, and we left the creek with Luke lying there. He could walk into town for all I cared. That curly wolf followed, and that's when I noticed that old leather collar I had made on his neck. That was my curly wolf! He left when Pa did but came back and found me.

Susan began to tell me what had happened.

"Luke came to the store earlier and told me that you had come back and was up at your old property. He said he would drive me out. So he went in the back and told my father where we were going, and I grabbed my hat."

"He told your father you were going on a picnic," I explained. "No," she said. "He said that you had sent for me and that you had been hurt and needed my help." The sun began to shine again, and we rode arm in arm back to town.

I left the buckboard with Herman and told him to let me know when Luke got back. He never did because Luke never came back, and just as well as I would have kilt him for wrestling Susan and throwing her on the ground, not to mention the knife he held to her pretty throat.

Susan and I walked hand in hand to the store. Her father welcomed us when we came in. Her father said, "Susan, you should give Andy what his father left here." She went behind the counter, and when she pulled it out, I almost busted out crying. It was my Ma's family Bible!

Susan told me, "Your Pa came in here and told my father that he needed some supplies to go to the gold camp. He had no money but pulled this Bible from out of his haversack and said could we hold it for him until he came back with some gold? He looked at me and said that he had a son about my age who was in town and that someday I could meet him."

Providence? My Pa gave Ma's Bible to the girl that I loved. I opened it up and read my mother's words on the flyleaf:

"The Bible is a book that stands alone. There never was, nor will there ever be, another book like it. As there is but one sun to enlighten the world naturally, so there is but one book to enlighten the world spiritually."

— Mary

The past days came cascading over my mind like that waterfall in the Telluride Valley. God had spared me from death and evil men. He gave me favor with Chief Ouray. A wolf and a horse watched over me, but there was something more. Now, I had riches, but I really did not know the God of the Bible like my Ma did.

I felt empty on the inside. That is when I knelt down in that general store in front of Susan and her father and God. I was the only son of Hugh and Mary Jackson. God only had one Son. I turned to the passage my Ma had marked and read to me every night before bed, and I read it out loud.

"For God so loved the world that he gave his only begotten Son, that whosoever believeth on him should not perish, but have everlasting life." St. John 3:16

I thought of how Henry Clay spent his whole life working and then died. What is the purpose of life? Looking back, I can see that the Lord was watching over me from Georgia to Colorado.

He spared me from freezing the first winter we had come here. He gave me friends like Boss Callahan and Thelma. I just happened to run into Henry Clay at the twilight of his life. Providence!

So I prayed my mother's prayer. How many times had she asked me to pray it with her? It came flooding back into my heart and mind, "Father, I believe that you raised your Son Jesus from the dead for me. I publicly confess with my mouth in front of Susan and her father that you forgive my sins, and I believe that in my heart. I receive Jesus Christ as my personal Savior today. Amen!"

I now was on the trail to somewhere!

AT THE END OF THE TRAIL

My father was a preacher, and he and my mother taught us boys to live a life that was pleasing to God. There was a song that Dad would sing when Mom played the piano on Sunday mornings in church.

> At the end of the trail
> Where dreams come true,
> We'll live forever
> In the home of the blue.
>
> Then, together, we'll roam
> 'Ore hill and vale,
> Just beyond the river
> At the end of the trail.
> —Vep Ellis

Many of my life's experiences were incorporated into this story. I have been to Colorado many times and found gold in a sluice in a mine for tourists to visit. I have slept at the foot of the Front Range and rode a train from Missouri to Colorado.

That same train took us to the top of the Rocky Mountains through Utah and down through Donner Pass to California. The story of the stream that was so clear that you could not judge the depth happened to me in Tunk Lake. I thought it was just a couple of feet deep, so I stepped in and went in over my head.

When I was younger, I explored caves in West Virginia and Indiana. They call it spelunking. One time, I got stuck in what they called the "Bardangus Hole." It was quite a time getting out and climbing back up on the rope. It was a close call as I got hyperthermia.

My great-uncle had an old sawmill in the woods of Maine, and I spent time exploring them. The outdoors always had a draw on my heart. The smell of pines stays with me whether it is in Maine or the piney woods of Texas. I have slept under the trees many times.

I have visited the First Nations reservations in Canada and the United States. They stand as a noble people in God's eyes. Whether I was in Arizona with the Apache, Oklahoma with the Cherokee, Maine with the Penobscot, or Florida with the Seminole, it was always a wonderful time for me to learn and observe.

My wife and I just got back from Canada, where we visited the Six Nations and also the Ojibwe at Kettle Point and Stoney Creek. We have many great friends among the First Nations.

The purpose of this book is to call for men to be men. We reject the tearing down of masculinity and call to boys to grow up with values that will make them great husbands and fathers. It is also a call to come to Christ and learn biblical values that will endure until you, and I get to the end of the trail!

EPILOGUE

The gulls swirled in the air, and the shores of the Virginia colony appeared in the mist that hung on the Chesapeake Bay. The James River spilled out into the bay, and the brackish tidewater was a mixture of the freshwater from the mountains and saltwater of the Atlantic.

A sailor in the masthead cried out, "Land ho!" Young Patrick lifted his eyes to see the new world. He had come to the bow of the ship earlier that morning in anticipation of being the first to see Jamestown. It was 1720 in the year of our Lord, and Jamestown had been a colony for over one hundred years. The Plymouth colony in New England would be one hundred years old in December.

Patrick had read a manuscript by Sir Walter Raleigh in the book stalls located on Thames Street in London Towne. He knew that the first settlers had landed here at Cape Henry on April 29, 1607. The stories he read of the New World had fired his imagination and gave him a desire to leave the filth of London and have a better life in the promised paradise of the Virginia colony.

His piercing blue eyes scanned the horizon, and he began to make out the homes with smoke drifting out of the chimneys as the inhabitants were stirring to greet this new day. Patrick, son of Jack, had begun an adventure that would start on these shores, but he would be drawn deeper into the continent by the far blue mountains.

The captain gave orders for all hands to come to the deck, and a sailor threw a knotted rope with lead on the end into the water. He was sounding for depth and called to the captain the fathoms and feet.

They had hit the channel, and the docks became visible as the ship caught one last draft of wind. The sails were dropped, and a small boat was launched. They had arrived in the Virginia colony.

Unbeknownst to him, the day would come that his great-grandson would carry the legacy of the son of Jack to the far western country. However, on this day,

Patrick, Jack's son, was ready to embark on a life that would be filled with peril and challenges that would take him into the vast wilderness that stretched before him.

Patrick felt the fowling pistol handle thrust into his belt. He knew he had a few gold sovereigns sewn into the lining of his coat. A bedroll contained his few worldly goods. A knife, a journal, a small pouch of lead balls for his pistol, and a few scraps of paper with his notes that he had copied in the book stalls about this country were all he had.

He had one more thing that was the most valuable of all: a map. He had found it among the manuscripts in the stalls. It was written and sketched by one James Hardesty, a soldier in His Majesty's service. It showed a trail leading from Jamestown, which started on the James River. Then, at the headwaters, Hardesty marked an X where he had landed his canoe.

It was not marked by leagues but by landmarks. The three mountains were marked the far blue mountains, and a pass was indicated that went through them into a great valley. There, a stream was sketched, and the words "silver rocks" were written.

In the early days of the colony, all discoveries of gold and silver went to the Virginia Company and ultimately to the King. A man was indentured to the company with the promise of lands upon the completion of his servitude. They were not allowed to keep any minerals or stones deemed precious. A violation of this led to a hand being chopped off or even hanging.

There were some sailors who would attempt to smuggle cargo into the colony and sell it to the settlers privately; this, too, was punishable by death for both parties involved.

The first Africans were brought ashore by sailors who had captured a Portuguese man of war off the Virginia coast. They were used to harvest tobacco crops and were given no rights or hope. One plantation owner had secretly bought these souls, but when the Governor of the colony found out, he allowed it for a share of the increased profits.

There was a foul mixture in the colony, and it was not just the smell of the tidewater where the river and the ocean met; it was also the mixture of the godly and the ungodly. Thus, the evil of slavery was born in the New World.

Patrick would soon owe his life to one of the African slaves, a majestic warrior from a Zulu tribe. Our story will see a great bond established and the seeds for all men to work together.

Patrick went ashore with the second boat. He could hardly contain his excitement. A soldier met them at the dock, and they were led to a table where they gave their names to be checked against the ship's roster.

The soldier eyed the document and then him and said, "Welcome, Patrick Jack's son!" Quarters in the Newtown were reserved for them until they got established. Patrick did not plan on staying long in this wooden hut.

He kept his possessions with him and began to explore his surroundings. He saw a tavern with the unlikely name of the Duck and Squirrel. The tavern keeper greeted him with a grunt. "Whatcha want?" Patrick saw the board had shepherd's pie on it for a tuppence. He laid his money down on the bar and ordered the shepherd's pie.

The tavern keeper slopped a ladle into a bowl none to clean and slid it over to him. "What's in it?" Patrick asked. "Duck and squirrel, the owner replied with a chuckle. It made him no matter as he was tired of the hard tack and water that had been his meal on the ship for the last week.

Patrick smelled the savory aroma, and his stomach welcomed this change in diet. He was here, safely across the Atlantic with no problems, and now sitting in a smoky tavern with a warm meal under his belt.

It was then he heard two men sitting behind him. "I tell you, there is treasure in those far mountains!" The other man snorted, "Not so loud." They both had been drinking, and the smell of rum filled Patrick's nostrils. The men began whispering, but Patrick decided right there and then that he would take out for the mountains tomorrow.

(THE SAGA BEGINS)

THE COLORADO TERRITORY (1861)

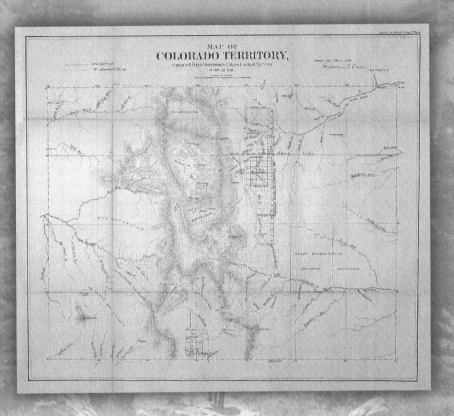

The federal government had constructed the boundaries, taking portions of land from Nebraska, Utah, Kansas, and New Mexico. It was a shrewd move to protect the resources of gold, silver, and lead for the Union.